Jane Austen's Pride & Prejudice: A Study Guide

Jane Austen's Pride and Prejudice: A Study Guide

Tracey Smith

2014

First Printing: 2014

ISBN 978-1-291-76377-5

ABOUT THE AUTHOR

Born on 16th December 1775, Jane Austen came from a large family. Austen's father was the rector for the parsonage of Steventon in Hampshire. Her mother was frequently ill, yet nevertheless had a lively mind and always enjoyed a joke.

Little is known of Jane's childhood, though it is known that she and her sister, Cassandra, were taught at home by their mother. In 1782 the girls stayed at Southampton with some relatives before moving to Oxford to continue their education with the widow of a principal of Brasenose College. Cassandra then went on to Abbey School in Reading and Jane followed her there shortly afterwards. Though Jane was too young for school, she could not bear to be separated from Cassandra. The girls' education away from home did not last long, with them returning home two years later.

One of Jane's nieces described Jane's appearance as:

> *The figure tall and slight, but not drooping; well-balanced, as was proved by her quick firm step. Her complexion of that rare sort which seems the particular property of light brunettes, a mottled skin, not fair, but perfectly clear and healthy; the fine naturally curling hair, neither light nor dark, the bright hazel eyes to match, and the rather small, but well-shaped nose.*

Jane was a quiet person, who preferred to listen to conversation, rather than participate. She began to write during her teenage years and commenced her first book in 1796. This book was sent to the publishers under the title *First Impressions* and was published sixteen years later with the title *Pride and Prejudice*.

SETTING OF THE NOVEL

The setting of *Pride and Prejudice* is within the society in which Jane Austen herself lived. The people within the book are wealthy enough to keep horses and carriages and to entertain their neighbours. Mrs Bennet herself emphasized this point when she said, *"I know that we dine with twenty-four families"*. This society may not have tolerated those people associated with trade, yet had no trouble accepting those that had made their fortune through trade. *Pride and Prejudice* is about the lives of people that Jane Austen's family was concerned with – the clergy and gentlefolk. In other words Austen wrote about what she knew.

Mrs Bennet's views on motherhood and money are probably representative of middle class societies during this time. While parental authority was firm at this time, Mr Bennet was not a good example of this given his inability to exert enough power over his daughters. Though he recognizes that Jane and Elizabeth are sensible enough not to need his parental guidance, he is wise enough to acknowledge that Lydia's foolish behaviour is directly related to his slack parenting ability. As a result, he becomes particularly firm of Lydia's trousseau when the time comes, which surprises his wife. The lessons he learnt from Lydia have a detrimental effect on his relationship with Kitty. This is evidenced when he says:

> *Kitty, I have at least learnt to be cautious, and you will feel the effects of it. No officer will enter my house again, or ever to pass through the village.*

It was the father that called the shots for the social and economic aspects of the family. As such, the Bennet ladies are unable to make the acquaintance of Mr Bingley until Mr Bennet had done so.

This is a society in which girls were not independent. They moved from their father's house to that of their husband's. Women were expected to be accomplished. Both Darcy and Bingley acknowledge the accomplishment of women, though it is Miss Bingley that summed up what is expected of an accomplished woman of this period:

> *A woman must have a thorough knowledge of music, singing, drawing, dancing and the modern languages to deserve the word; and besides all this she must possess a certain something in her air and manner of walking.*

WHAT HAPPENS IN THE NOVEL

Pride and Prejudice is set in a Hertfordshire Village named Longbourn not far from the market town of Meryton. Mr Bennet has a small estate which will go to a distant cousin – a clergyman named Mr Collins upon his death. He and his wife have five daughters, Jane, Elizabeth, Lydia, Mary and Kitty. With the exception of Mary, each of the Bennet girls regard marriage as the primary goal.

The arrival of Mr Bingley, the new tenant of Netherfield Park, causes great excitement and Mrs Bennet is enthusiastic about her husband making the acquaintance of the newcomer. Mr Bingley eventually does so, establishing a relationship with the Mr Bingley, who soon introduces his friend, Mr Darcy, who is aloof, though very wealthy.

At about the same time, the militia move into the neighbouring town, much to the delight of Lydia and Kitty. The two girls manage to meet with the young officers while staying with the aunt, Mrs Phillips. On one of their visits they meet a newly-appointed officer, George Wickham.

While in the company of the Bennet girls, Darcy and Wickham meet and their dislike for one another is evident immediately. The dislike of one another stems from a disagreement on instructions given to Wickham's dying father in regards to allowing him to enter the church.

Shortly after this meeting Elizabeth is forced to spend time in the company of Darcy at Netherfield Park, where the two of them engage in intellectual sparring. Darcy comes to find Elizabeth stimulating, and despite his distaste for her inferior social status, he finds himself falling in love with her. Elizabeth is staying at Netherfield to tend to Jane who is there after falling ill during a visit with Mr Bingley's sisters. Bingley's love for Jane is evident in his attentiveness to her during her convalescence. Caroline Bingley does not approve of the match and is hoping that her brother will marry Darcy's sister Georgina. At the same time, Elizabeth finds Wickham to be a pleasant companion, though will not allow her feelings to grow too strong.

The Bennet family receive a surprise visit from Mr Collins who is the heir to Mr Bennet's property and Elizabeth is surprised to receive a marriage proposal from him. He does not accept her refusal and appeals to Mr Bennet in order to change her mind. Mr Bennet surprised Mr Collins by refusing to promote the idea of marriage, despite Mrs Bennet's insistence that the marriage would be an ideal union. Mr Collins, shortly afterwards, marries Charlotte Lucas, one of Elizabeth's closest friends. At first, Elizabeth is greatly disappointed, thinking that Charlotte must be disappointed by her choice in husband; yet after visiting the couple at their home at Hunsford Parsonage, she finds that the marriage is a pleasant one.

Elizabeth travels to Hunsford with Mr Lucas and Charlotte's sister on the way to London where she stays with the Gardiners (her aunt and uncle). The Bingleys are in London at the same time and Elizabeth is concerned over the fact that Mr Bingley makes no effort to visit with Jane.

Hunsford is near Rosings Park where Lady Catherine de Bourgh lives, Mr Darcy's aunt whom Mr Collins is subservient to. Mr Darcy and Colonel Fitzwilliam – another of Lady Catherine's nephews – are spending time with their aunt and meet Elizabeth regularly. On one of their meetings, Colonel Fitzwilliam tells Elizabeth that Bingley is intentionally avoiding Jane on Darcy's advice. Darcy does what he can to convince Bingley that Jane's lower social status was not appropriate for him, with the addition of a gossiping mother and irresponsible younger sisters, the family was altogether undesirable. Having found out all this information, Elizabeth is furious and in letting her anger be known, Darcy confesses his love for Elizabeth. She is scornful in her rejection of Darcy and she berates him for treating Wickham badly and separating Bingley and Jane. In his anger, Darcy leaves Elizabeth, but once he has gone Elizabeth begins to reconsider her opinion of Darcy.

The following morning Darcy gives Elizabeth a letter, which not only provides disparaging remarks about the Bennet family, but also gives a full and detailed account of Wickham's misdemeanours and proof of his lying and deceitful ways. After much consideration, Elizabeth comes to significant conclusions about Wickham's worthlessness and acknowledges that many of the remarks about her own family are correct. The letter leaves Elizabeth feeling very sorry for the way she has treated Darcy.

Shortly after this, Lydia is invited to stay with the wife of Colonel Forster. Lydia gladly accepts, believing that it will provide her with more opportunities to see the officers before they leave Meryton. Lydia's trip upsets Kitty and gives Elizabeth a longing to get away, who in turn accepts an invitation to holiday with the Gardiners in Derbyshire.

The Gardiners and Elizabeth visit Pemberley – the Darcy estate – but are advised of the absence of Mr Darcy. While looking about the property, they come face to face with Darcy who arrived home unexpectedly. All parties are embarrassed at the meeting and after abruptly addressing Elizabeth, Mr Darcy hurries off. Shortly afterwards Darcy returns and asks that Elizabeth introduce him to the Gardiners and ask that they all return to meet his sister and the Bingley's.

While Caroline Bingley is quite rude to the visitors, Darcy, his sister and Mr Bingley are all very polite and Elizabeth comes to recognize many of Darcy's good qualities. When Darcy finds Elizabeth one day grief-stricken over the news of Lydia's elopement with Wickham, he finds it difficult to say the right thing to her and as a consequence she believes Lydia's behaviour has formed another barrier between the two of them that can never be resolved.

Darcy and Mr Gardiner find Lydia and bribe Wickham into marrying Lydia. The Bennet family are under the impression that this was all the doing of Mr Gardiner, though in time Elizabeth finds it was the sole responsibility of Mr Darcy.

Shortly afterwards Bingley and Jane become engaged, Elizabeth receives a visit from Lady Catherine de Bough who accuses her of trying to marry Mr Darcy for his money. After a misunderstanding is cleared up about the couple's intentions towards one another, Darcy and Elizabeth become engaged and after the two sisters marry and live near one another in Derbyshire.

CHAPTER SUMMARY

Chapter 1: Mr and Mrs Bennet are discussing the arrival of a wealthy new neighbour. Mrs Bennet is enthusiastic for her husband to make Mr Bingley's acquaintance in the hope that he may fall in love and marry one of their five daughters. She is also eager to have their introductions made before Sir William and Lady Lucas do.

This chapter introduces many of the important themes within *Pride and Prejudice*. One of the most quoted lines – *'It is a truth universally acknowledged that a single man in possession of a good fortune, must be in want of a wife'* – underlines the importance of marrying well within the society that is represented in this novel.

Mrs Bennet is portrayed as a silly old woman who relies on her frail nerves to get what she wants, but it is clear she is the intellectual equal of her husband, who greatly dislikes her. This chapter gives us an insight into a marriage gone sour.

Chapter 2: Mr Bennet pays a visit to Mr Bingley, but does not tell his wife about it. He refuses to tell her about the trip until her frustration is at a peak which gives him great delight. Upon finding out that Mr Bennet has in fact made the acquaintance of Mr Bingley his wife and daughters are delighted. The revelation produces Mr Bennet's desired effect, which is the bewilderment and benevolence of his family. This chapter is evidence of Mrs Bennet's competitiveness.

Chapter 3: Mr Bennet is bombarded with questions about Mr Bingley, though he is unwilling to answer any of them, leaving the Bennet ladies to find out more from their neighbour, Lady Lucas. Their interest in Mr Bingley is satisfied within a few days when he repays Mr Bennet's visit. He is invited to dinner which he initially accepts, but later must decline. His inability to attend the dinner causes Mrs Bennet concern that he is not as settled as she'd wish. However, Lady Lucas advises Mrs Bennet that he has gone to

London in order to arrange a party to attend the upcoming ball in Meryton. There is much concern shown for the party, most particularly the ladies that it will include. Once the evening arrives, however, it is found that the party only includes Mr Bingley, his two sisters, his brother-in-law – Mr Hurst – and his friend, Mr Darcy.

At the ball, Mr Bingley is discovered to be a lively and friendly person. He dances with all the girls, yet he pays particular attention to Jane. His friend, Mr Darcy, though is considered aloof and quite rude. He is dismissive of Elizabeth and refers to her as *"tolerable, but not handsome enough"*. Elizabeth recounts the episode to her friends later. Upon returning home, Mrs Bennet tells her husband how the evening went and of how Mr Bingley favoured Jane. She described Mr Darcy as a *"a most disagreeable, horrid man"*.

Mrs Bennet's desire to see her daughters marry well is palpable in this chapter. She says she will *"have nothing to wish for"* should she be able to marry Jane off to Mr Bingley and the other girls to gentlemen. Her desire to see her daughters marry well is given reason in chapter seven when the reader learns that Mr Bennet's property is entailed to Mr Collins. The introduction of Mr Darcy is an important point in the book. His personality is in stark contrast to that of Mr Bingley. The themes of the novel – pride and prejudice – are established in this chapter.

Chapter 4: Jane and Elizabeth discuss the evening. Elizabeth is pleased about Jane's feelings towards Mr Bingley and his sisters. However, Elizabeth finds Mr Bingley's sisters to be *"proud and conceited"*. Mr Bingley's wealth is considered below Mr Darcy's due to it being acquired by trade, where as Mr Darcy's is family money.

This chapter serves to emphasis the closeness between Jane and Elizabeth, but also highlights the most significant difference between them; Jane only sees the good in others, yet Elizabeth is more critical.

Chapter 5: This chapter introduces the Lucas family – close friends of the Bennets. Sir William Lucas, who made his fortune through trade, was knighted as a result of an address he made to the King. His wife, Lady Lucas, is a good friend of Mrs Bennet and their daughter, Charlotte is close friends with Elizabeth. The Bennets visit the Lucas family to talk over the ball and Charlotte tells of how she over-heard Mr Bingley commenting that Jane was the *"prettiest"* girl in the room. Again, Mr Darcy is found to be most disagreeable.

This chapter includes another reference to social distinctions, reminding the reader of the class-conscious society in which the novel is based.

Chapter 6: The Bennet ladies visit Netherfield Park and in due course, the visit is reciprocated. Miss Bingley and Mrs Hurst are impressed with Jane and Elizabeth, however, find that Mrs Bennet and the Lydia and Kitty are *"not worth speaking to"*. It becomes very clear that Mr Bingley is attracted to Jane and Charlotte expresses her concern that Jane is restrained in showing her emotions and fears that Bingley may not appreciate the depth of her affection for him. At one stage during the ball, Darcy finds himself standing near Elizabeth and surprises himself to find that he is interested in her. Sir William encourages the two of them to dance, but Elizabeth refuses.

This chapter introduces Elizabeth's views on marriage and she is greatly mistaken in thinking her friend Charlotte shares similar views. However, Charlotte's age and position in society has given her a more pragmatic and less idealistic view of marriage. While Elizabeth considers love, rather than security, to be the primary force behind a good marriage, Charlotte is more cynical. This chapter also provides an interesting turn of events for Elizabeth and Darcy's relationship. He acknowledges that he appreciates her beauty and intelligence, but Elizabeth deflects his initial attempts at courting her as she misjudges his attentions. Her bad mannered refusal to dance with him, however, does not put Darcy off, but in fact provides him an example of her great spirit that he finds attractive.

Chapter 7: In this chapter, the reader gains an understanding of the financial situation of the Bennet family. We learn that Mr Bennet's fortune is entailed to a distant male relative as he has no sons of his own that may inherit his property, Longbourn. The reader learns that Mrs Bennet has a sister living in the nearby Meryton – Mrs Phillips. Kitty and Lydia visit their aunt while shopping. Mr and Mrs Phillips have strong ties with the militia that are currently stationed nearby.

Jane receives a letter from Caroline Bingley requesting her to join her at Netherfield. Mrs Bennet arranges for her to travel by horseback, aware that it will probably rain and therefore be forced to stay at Netherfield. While travelling over there, Jane gets soaked and catches a cold and is forced to stay there until she recovers. Elizabeth insists on visiting her there, and walks through the mud arriving dishevelled and dirty to the shock and disgrace of Miss Bingley and Mrs Hurst; though Darcy is in admiration of what the walk does for Elizabeth's complexion. A doctor advises Jane that she is to stay in bed to recuperate and Elizabeth begrudgingly accepts Miss Bingley's and Mrs Hursts' offer to stay to help with her sister's recovery.

Chapter 8: Over dinner, Elizabeth's dislike of Miss Bingley and Mrs Hurst is heightened by the fact that once Jane is out of sight, she is as good as forgotten about. Elizabeth chooses to escape from the dinner table as early as possible to see Jane. After Elizabeth leaves, the sisters engage in a scornful conversation about Elizabeth's appearance, while both Mr Darcy and Mr Bingley defend the girls and their family. Elizabeth returns to the library and overhears the conversation.

This chapter emphasises that Elizabeth has more accurate impression of Miss Bingley and Mrs Hurst than does her sister.

The ridiculing of Elizabeth is evidently motivated by jealousy and snobbery which leads the reader to judge Miss Bingley and Mrs Hurst quite harshly. This is the author's way of approaching small mindedness and it is clear that Austen believes Elizabeth to be a valuable model of womanhood. This chapter also establishes the compatibility of Mr Darcy and Elizabeth – they share not just their love of reading, but personal qualities such as pride, intelligence and honesty.

Chapter 9: Elizabeth writes to her mother requesting that she comes to visit in order to assess Jane's condition. Mrs Bennet arrives with Kitty and Lydia in tow and finds that Jane is not as ill as she had feared. Mrs Bennet and Mr Darcy have a conversation about the merits of town versus country life; a conversation in which – true to her nature – Mrs Bennet makes several stupid remarks which results in her being treated with contempt. In this chapter, Elizabeth sees her as Mr Darcy views her as an interfering and socially inept woman, which upsets her. Elizabeth does what she can to change the subject.

Chapter 10: The following day is spent in leisurely pursuits such as writing letters and playing cards. Elizabeth, Bingley and Darcy get involved in a discussion about humility and changing opinions. Elizabeth becomes aware of Darcy's growing interest in her, but infers his request for a dance as an opportunity to mock her and therefore refuses him.

This chapter serves to emphasis the differences between the characters of Bingley and Darcy, however it also serves to highlight the similarities between Elizabeth and Darcy. To the reader only, does Darcy's feelings towards Elizabeth become evident.

Chapter 11: Jane is well enough to join everyone after dinner. Mr Bingley makes a fuss over Jane. Miss Bingley tries to gain the attention of Mr Darcy but to no avail. Darcy and Elizabeth enter into a discussion about one another's faults. In this chapter

Bingley's obvious interest in Jane is met with Elizabeth's approval, while Darcy's growing interest in Elizabeth is met with Caroline Bingley's serious disapproval.

Chapter 12: Elizabeth writes to her mother requesting a carriage to bring them home but is met with her refusal to do so, putting Elizabeth in a position to have to ask Bingley for transport home. Bingley agrees and the girls return home on Sunday. Mrs Bennet is not happy at their return home, though their father is glad to see them.

Chapter 13: Mr Bennet tells his family of a letter he received from Mr Collins – the heir to his estate – advising that he will be coming, and is to arrive the following day. Mr Bennet is most amused by the letter, describing it as *"a mixture of servility and self-importance . . . which promises well."* When Mr Collins arrives he is in great admiration of Mr Bennet's daughters, indicating the true intent of his visit. Elizabeth's perception of Mr Collins, developed through reading his letter, is confirmed upon meeting him.

Chapter 14: Mr Bennet asks about Lady Catherine de Bough, Mr Collins' patroness. Mr Collins describes her in glowing terms and Mr Bennet discovers that *"his cousin was absurd as he hoped"* – a belief he shares with Elizabeth. Mr Collins reads from Fordyce's Sermons but Lydia's constant interruptions offend him. This chapter establishes Mr Collins' absurd personality with his exaggerated formality, insincerity and his mockingly humble arrogance.

Chapter 15: This chapter sees Mr Collins begin his pursuit of a wife. His first choice is Jane, however Mrs Bennet makes it clear that she believes Jane to be soon engaged to Mr Bingley. It does not take time for him to turn his attention to Elizabeth.

The girls, with the exception of Mary, and Mr Collins walk to Meryton where they meet Officers Denny and Wickham. Bingley and Darcy arrive at about the same time and Elizabeth notices the tension between Mr Darcy and Officer Wickham. The girls and Mr Collins go on to visit Mrs Phillips – the girls' aunt – who invites them to dinner the following day.

Chapter 16: Mr Wickham joins the dinner party at Mrs Phillips' the following day and while the dinner guests are playing cards, Wickham tells Elizabeth that Mr Darcy has treated him badly. Wickham explains to Elizabeth that Darcy's father had promised him a good living within the church, though when the time came the younger Mr Darcy refused to follow through on the bequest. Elizabeth is appropriately outraged on hearing this story, and she later finds out that Lady Catherine de Bough is in fact Darcy's aunt.

Chapter 17: Elizabeth retells Wickham's story to Jane who finds it difficult to believe. All is soon forgotten though when they are invited to a ball at Netherfield the following week. The days leading up to the ball are rainy and windy putting a stop to the girls leaving the house. Mr Collins greatly looks forward to the dance and asks Elizabeth for two dances – much to her great annoyance. His comments lead her to believe that he may wish to marry her.

Chapter 18: Wickham does not attend the ball at Netherfield, Elizabeth presumes this is because of Darcy's presence. Darcy asks Elizabeth to dance and she consents. During the dance, Elizabeth picks up that Sir Lucas expects there to be an engagement between Bingley and Jane very soon and Darcy discovers that Elizabeth sympathizes with Wickham. Later in the evening, Mr Collins makes himself look foolish when introducing himself to Darcy. Mrs Bennet is extremely rude about Darcy within his earshot. Mary embarrasses herself by boring everyone with her singing; as does Mr Collins giving a long speech about why he does not sing. To make it worse, their carriage is late and it is made very clear they are overstaying their welcome.

Chapter 19: Mrs Bennet and Mr Collins conspire to have Mr Collins a private conversation with Elizabeth where he asks her to marry him. He explains his reasons, among them, him being a clergymen he will be able to provide a sufficient income. He tells Elizabeth that he is understanding of her having little money but would not reproach her for that. Elizabeth finally interrupts his monologue to refuse his offer. As a result of his ego, Mr Collins believes Elizabeth is being coy and tells her that they have the consent of both of her parents, believing this will change her mind. Elizabeth has trouble convincing him of her refusal, so appeals to her father for help.

Chapter 20: Mrs Bennet gets very upset at hearing the news that Elizabeth has declined Mr Collins' offer of marriage and goes on to insist that her husband change her mind. Mr Bennet talks to Elizabeth and upon finding her adamant about not marrying Mr Collins, he tells her that her mother refuses to see her again if she refuses; however, her father will have nothing to do with her should she accept.

Chapter 21: Elizabeth hopes that Mr Collins will depart immediately following her refusal of marriage, however he seems determined to say for the remainder of his holiday. Jane receives a letter from Caroline Bingley advising her that her family has gone to London and don't plan to return for a very long time. Caroline also writes that her brother Charles is fond of Georgina (Darcy's sister) and expects to hear of their engagement soon. Jane is very upset at this news, but refuses to think ill of Caroline, despite Elizabeth believing they have gone to London because Caroline wants to separate Jane and her brother.

Chapter 22: Mr Collins asks Charlotte Lucas to marry him and she agrees. Charlotte's family is very happy, however Elizabeth is shocked and believes Charlotte will be very unhappy in her choice of husband. This chapter highlights Charlotte's pragmatic view of marriage which is in stark contrast to that of her friend Elizabeth's view of marriage. Charlotte's choice to marry a man for security, rather than for romantic reasons, is the realistic side of the society within Jane Austen lives. Charlotte's solution to her current social situation is a practical response to a need to protect herself within a patriarchal society.

Chapter 23: Sir Lucas visits the Bennet family in order to announce the engagement of Charlotte and Mr Collins. Mrs Bennet is resentful of the news and takes the opportunity to tell him that Elizabeth was, in fact, his first choice. Mrs Bennet blames Elizabeth for the situation and refuses to forgive her. Lady Lucas calls over to Longbourn regularly to tell Mrs Bennet how happy she is about the engagement. Mr Collins' return to the Bennet household is greeted rather coolly, however he spends much of his time at the Lucas Lodge. Mrs Bennet is upset over the idea of Charlotte become the future mistress of Longbourn.

While, to the reader, the engagement between Mr Collins and Charlotte is a reasonable idea, one can also understand why Mrs Bennet might be upset. She is concerned about ensuring her daughters are married and receives no help from her husband in this area. Upon the death of Mr Bennet, his daughters will have little financial support, therefore making a successful marriage very important for each of the girls. It is evident that Charlotte's decision to marry Mr Collins, at the age of 27, is largely based on the same motivations of financial dependence. The lack of suitable men for the Bennet girls to marry is seen at the Meryton Assembly, when Elizabeth is forced to sit out a dance.

Chapter 24: Miss Bingley writes to Jane to advise that they have established themselves in London for the winter. In the letter,

Miss Bingley tells of the virtues of Georgiana Darcy and infers that she is the choice of Mr Bingley for a wife. Jane is upset and believes she has made "an error of fancy" about a future between herself and Mr Bingley. Elizabeth disagrees and believes that Miss Bingley is doing everything she can to separate her sister from Mr Bingley. They turn the topic of conversation to the marriage of Charlotte and Mr Collins. The sisters have very different views on the marriage. Elizabeth can only condemn the union, while Jane is far more understanding of Charlotte's predicament and can therefore understand her decision to marry Mr Collins.

Chapter 25: Mr Collins leaves. Mr and Mrs Gardiner arrive. Mrs Gardiner is Jane and Elizabeth's favourite relative and she invites Jane to stay with her in London. Mrs Gardiner also advises Elizabeth against Wickham, having viewed them together socially. Mrs Gardiner's calming personality is a welcome relief at Longbourn and is in stark contrast to that of Mrs Bennet. Her views on the romance of Jane and Mr Bingley are practical and is wise to Elizabeth and Jane's differing views on romance.

Chapter 26: Mrs Gardiner expresses her concern about Elizabeth's affections for Wickham, and warns her that "the want of fortune would make so very imprudent." Elizabeth does admit that she is not in love with Wickham but money would not influence her choice in a future husband. Mr Collins returns for the wedding and Charlotte asks her to visit her the following March. After the wedding Mr Collins and Charlotte leave for Kent. Jane, who is in London, writes to Elizabeth telling her of Miss Bingley's rudeness and attempts at avoiding her. Elizabeth writes to Mrs Gardiner telling her how Wickham is now romantically attached to Miss King, who has a small fortune of her own.

Elizabeth shows her vulnerability when she almost succumbs to the charms of Wickham and her financial situation saved her from becoming a serious target for his affection. Jane is the epitome of morality in this chapter and she acknowledges that Elizabeth was correct in her assessment of Miss Bingley.

Chapter 27: Elizabeth stops over in London on her way to Hunsford with Sir William and Maria Lucas. Elizabeth visits with Charlotte. In discussion with her aunt about marriage, Jane and Wickham, Elizabeth takes on a cynical view of marriage which she uses to cover her disappointment in Wickham's announcement of his impending marriage. Elizabeth is invited to go to the Lake District with the Gardiners.

Elizabeth's cynicism is not taken seriously in this chapter, however the reasons for it are real. She has genuine concern about marrying someone she does not love simply for financial security.

Chapter 28: Elizabeth arrives at Hunsford with the Lucases and are shown around by Charlotte and Mrs Collins. Elizabeth notices Charlotte's embarrassment of her husband's effusiveness, however does believe that she is, by and large, happy. Miss Anne de Bourgh and Mrs Jenkinson offer an invitation to dinner and Elizabeth believes Anne to be a "proper wife" for Darcy.

The advantages of Charlotte's marriage to Mr Collins are evident in this chapter. Charlotte deals with her boring husband by largely ignoring him and encouraging him to spend time outside of the house.

Chapter 29: The dinner invitation causes concern for Mr Collins as he is anxious about how his guests will feel in the company of Lady Catherine who "likes to have the distinction of rank preserved." It turns out Elizabeth is the only one to feel herself up to the occasion, with Mrs Lucas being rather frightened and Sir William over-awed. Lady Catherine's demeanour only serves to confirm Wickham's assessment of her to Elizabeth, particularly after the judgements she makes of Elizabeth's family.

Lady Catherine's attitude is largely based on the belief that money and position equates to personal worth and provides the reader with the opportunity to judge her. Lady Catherine's judgement on the Bennet girls' lack of education and accomplishments only highlights that Elizabeth possesses better manner and education than does Lady Catherine.

Chapter 30: Sir William leaves Hunsford a week after arriving. Elizabeth, Charlotte and Mrs Lucas are kept up to date with what is happening at Lady Catherine's home by Mr Collins and they all dine together about twice a week. Mr Darcy and Colonel Fitzwilliam, Darcy's cousin, arrive at Rosings and visit the parsonage. Elizabeth asks Mr Darcy if he has seen Jane while in London, and he is embarrassed to admit that he hasn't.

Elizabeth's dislike of Mr Darcy, while fuelled by her first encounter with him, is strengthened by her belief that he is responsible for separating Jane and Mr Bingley. This chapter see Elizabeth misreading Mr Darcy's character, while unaware of his growing feelings towards her.

Chapter 31: As a result of the arrival of Mr Darcy and Colonel Fitzwilliam, Mrs Lucas, the Collins and Elizabeth are not required to be at Rosings for close to a week. When they do visit again, Elizabeth and Darcy get into a conversation about manners and she teases him about his manners at the dance at the Meryton Assembly.

This chapter further emphasises Darcy's growing interest in Elizabeth and her lively and engaging personality also peaks Fitzwilliam's interest in her. As a result of her feelings towards Darcy, Elizabeth is unable to see how he feels about her, which Austen uses to provide some heightened tension in the novel.

Chapter 32: Darcy interrupts Elizabeth while writing letters. Elizabeth uses the opportunity to question Darcy about why Mr Bingley left Netherfield so quickly. He doesn't answer and swiftly changes the topic of conversation to the Collinses' marriage. Darcy departs upon the arrival of Charlotte, though he continues to visit

Elizabeth with no apparent reason. Charlotte sees his visits for what they are and suggests to Elizabeth that Darcy is in love with her. A fact that Elizabeth vehemently disagrees with. Elizabeth is puzzled at Fitzwilliam's reticence around her, though it is a result of Fitzwilliam noticing Darcy's change of behaviour around Elizabeth.

Chapter 33: Elizabeth's walks are interrupted by Darcy, who makes indirect references to her staying at Rosings on future visits. She interprets this as Darcy believing her to have a future with Colonel Fitzwilliam, but later meets with Fitzwilliam where he tells of his necessity to marry well because of his "younger son status". Elizabeth also learns, that Fitzwilliam and Darcy, hold dual guardianship of Georgiana Darcy and Fitzwilliam divulged the role Darcy played in saving Mr Bingley from "a most imprudent marriage." Elizabeth is most upset at hearing this, believing that Jane is the one he refers to.

Chapter 34: Elizabeth re-reads Jane's letters and finds herself saddened by the thought that Darcy has caused her pain. While reading these letters, Darcy appears and confesses to being in love with her despite what he believes her social inferiority. His manner while professing his love is insulting to Elizabeth ane she is further insulted by his assumption that she will accept his proposal of marriage. Her refusal of his offer angers Darcy and is reproachful in her inability to be more civil under the circumstances. Darcy does not deny separating Bingley and Jane but is surprised to find that Elizabeth would have refused his offer despite this.

Darcy's proposal of marriage is a turning point in the novel. While Elizabeth may well be flattered, her anger and pride takes over, particularly given Darcy's poor timing.

Chapter 35: Elizabeth takes a walk near the park and is met by Darcy who gives her a letter to read. In the letter, he gives his version of the Jane and Mr Bingley affair and tells her of his account of Wickham.

This chapter, for the first time, allows the reader to see things from the viewpoint of Mr Darcy. It is also the first time we view Darcy on his own and not through the perspective of Elizabeth. The story of Wickham and his attempted elopement with Darcy's fifteen year old sister Georgiana is particularly important to the story as it explains Darcy's treatment of Wickham and puts him in the role of compassionate older brother.

Chapter 36: Initially, Elizabeth is critical of the contents of the letter, yet she does come around and finds that she has been "blind, partial, prejudiced, absurd." Elizabeth becomes aware that she has been unfair in her assessment of Darcy. Upon her return to the house, she finds that Mr Darcy and Colonel Fitzwilliam have been by to bid their farewell to the Collins family.

Elizabeth is humbled by the letter and is forced to re-evaluate not just the past events but also her reactions to them. It is refreshing to find in this chapter that Elizabeth is honest in her re-examination of her actions and conscience.

Chapter 37: Colonel Fitzwilliam and Darcy depart from Rosings and Lady Catherine's boredom means that she requires company from the Collinses, Elizabeth and Mrs Lucas. Elizabeth spends time reflecting on Darcy's letter and comes to the realization that the conduct of her family has been less than desirable. Elizabeth believes that she was right to decline Darcy's offer, she does become more compassionate towards him.

This chapter finds a wiser Elizabeth, who finds that she is better able to judge the personality of others, particularly that of her own family.

Chapter 38: Elizabeth and Mrs Lucas depart and Mr Collins tells Elizabeth that is welcome to visit any time. He tells her that he wishes she has a marriage as happy as his own and Elizabeth is surprised to find that Charlotte seems so content with her marriage to Mr Collins. Elizabeth's reflections on Charlotte's marriage remind us there is more to a successful marriage than love. It is clear that the author's sentiments about marriage are similar to that of Elizabeth's.

Chapter 39: Once Elizabeth arrives home, she learns the militia are departing for Brighton. Miss King has gone to Liverpool without Wickham. Lydia is keen to follow the Militia to Brighton and her immaturity is evident in the stories she relates to Jane and Elizabeth about how she has been spending her time. Mrs Bennet is also keen on the idea of spending the summer in Brighton, though her husband is not interested.

Chapter 40: Elizabeth tells Jane of Darcy's marriage proposal and the letter he wrote her about Wickham. While Jane is sympathetic to Darcy's feelings for Elizabeth, she is not so quick to denounce Wickham. Mrs Bennet questions Elizabeth extensively about the Collinses. In this chapter Elizabeth has chosen not to say anything about Wickham's behaviour to her family which in turn has consequences for them all. Elizabeth's decision not to say anything largely stems from her strong belief that she is behaving honourably towards him and is evidence of her unsophisticated knowledge of men.

Chapter 41: Kitty and Lydia are sad to see the regiment leave and Lydia is invited to Brighton by Mrs Forster, much to Kitty's displeasure. Elizabeth expresses her concern to her father and asks him not to her Lydia go. Mr Bennet disagrees with Elizabeth as he believes that Lydia will find that there are so many girls in Brighton, she may well be neglected. Wickham is unhappy to find that Elizabeth believes Darcy 'improves on acquaintance', though he suggests that he improves solely due to his affection for Miss de Bourgh.

Chapter 42: Elizabeth is unhappy at home with her mother constantly complaining. Kitty looks forward to visiting the Lakes and is disappointed when the date of departure must change due to business commitments of Mr Gardiner's. With a change of plans, the Gardiners take Elizabeth to Derbyshire and Mrs Gardiner suggests visiting Pemberley, Darcy's estate. Elizabeth is not keen on the idea until she finds that the family will not be there and is interested in seeing the house.

Chapter 43: Elizabeth greatly enjoys her visit to Pemberley and finds the house to be beautifully decorated. Mrs Reynolds – the Darcy's housekeeper – shows the guests around the house and in doing so points out Wickham's portrait and tells them that he has "become very wild." Mrs Reynolds affection for Mr Darcy and his sister, Georgina, is obvious and as the Gardiners and Elizabeth are leaving the property Darcy unexpectedly arrives much to his and Elizabeth's embarrassment. Later on, Darcy joins the visitors on the grounds and invites Mr Gardiner to fish in his stream. He tells the group that the Bingley's are coming to visit and would also like the Gardiners and Elizabeth to meet his sister when she arrives. Elizabeth is pleased that he wants her to become acquainted with his sister.

Chapter 44: Darcy, his sister and Bingley visit the Gardiners and Elizabeth. Elizabeth likes Georgina Darcy, finding her pleasant, unaffected and rather shy. The Gardiners are interested in Georgina's attitude towards Elizabeth. This is also the Gardiners first meeting of Mr Bingley. Everyone is invited to Pemberley for dinner.

Chapter 45: Georgina greets the visitors in her usual shy, but polite manner. Mrs Hurst and Miss Bingley, however, are barely civil. Mr Darcy is encouraging the development of a relationship between his sister and Elizabeth. Caroline Bingley does not like the turn of the conversation and asks Elizabeth what effect the absence of the militia is having on her family. After Mrs Gardiner and Elizabeth leave Caroline takes the opportunity to demean Elizabeth's *"person, behaviour and dress"*. Georgina does not get involved in the conversation as she trusts her brother's opinion more so than Caroline's.

Chapter 46: Elizabeth receives a letter from Jane telling her about Lydia's elopement with Wickham. A second letter arrives bringing news that Wickham has no intention of marrying Lydia. Darcy comes into the room and Elizabeth tells him why she is upset. Darcy is unhappy at hearing the news, believing he could have prevented the situation had he told the Bennet family of Wickham earlier. Elizabeth returns to Longbourn with the Gardiners.

Chapter 47: Elizabeth gets home to find that her father is in London searching for Lydia. Mrs Bennet is beside herself with grief and Mr Gardiner makes plans to return to London to assist Mr Bennet in his search for Lydia. Mary takes the opportunity, over dinner, to talk about morality and the loss of virtue. Lady Lucas, somewhat inappropriately, sends her condolences.

Chapter 48: Mr Bennet does not keep in regular contact, but the Bennet family hear from Mr Gardiner that they have, as yet, had no success in locating Lydia. They also receive a letter from Mr Collins who gives moralistic advice on how to deal with Lydia. Mr Bennet returns from London, having failed to locate his daughter.

Chapter 49: Two days later, Mr Gardiner writes to confirm he has found Lydia and for a guaranteed small income, Wickham has agreed to marry her. Mr Bennet agrees, despite his distress at the amount of money and believes the marriage a better option than Lydia's reputation ruined. Mrs Bennet, however, believes that Lydia is fortunate to be married at the age of sixteen.

Chapter 50: Mr Bennet regrets not having saved more money so that he could pay Wickham's debts and for the money for his marriage to Lydia, rather than being in debt to Mr Gardiner. Mrs Bennet begins looking for houses Lydia and Wickham to live in once they are married. Elizabeth regrets confiding in Darcy and believes he will be happy of her refusal in his marriage proposal once he finds Wickham to be her future brother in law.

Chapter 51: Lydia and Wickham arrive and evidently feel no shame or regret. As a married woman, Lydia is considered of greater importance in her mother's eyes. While at Longbourn, Lydia spends her time visiting people and attending parties. As a result she spends little time with her sisters. Lydia promises her mother that she will help find husbands for her sisters. It becomes clear to Elizabeth that Lydia is more in love with Wickham than he is with her. Lydia tells Elizabeth that Mr Darcy was present at the wedding.

Chapter 52: Mrs Gardiner writes to Elizabeth and tells her that Darcy paid off Wickham's gambling debts and provided him a position with in the army, along with a thousand pounds for the married couple. This was largely done because he felt guilty about not warning the family about Wickham's character. Elizabeth is surprised at the work Darcy has put into ensuring the marriage goes ahead and secretly believes he has in fact done it for her but does not understand to what end. Elizabeth firmly believes that Lydia's marriage has put a stop to any potential relationship between herself and Darcy. Wickham enters the room while Elizabeth is reading the letter and asks her about her visit to Darcy's estate at Pemberley.

Chapter 53: Lydia and her husband leave and the Bennets learn that Mr Bingley is to return to Netherfield. Not long after their return, Mr Bingley and Mr Darcy visit Longbourn; though

Mrs Bennet is quite rude much to the embarrassment of her guest and two eldest daughters.

Chapter 54: Mr Bingley and Mr Darcy attend a dinner party at Longbourn. Jane spends a lot of time with Mr Bingley and they both appear to greatly enjoy one another's company; however Darcy and Elizabeth spend little time with one another. It is evident that Elizabeth's frustration with the situation stems from her desire to recapture the intimacy she experienced with Darcy at Pemberley. She is, however, happy to see Jane and Bingley's relationship rekindled.

Chapter 55: Mr Bingley comes to visit a few days later, after Darcy has returned to London for ten days. He begins to visit with Jane regularly, and Mr Bennet says of him that he has *"nothing of presumption or folly"*, which for Mr Bennet, is high praise indeed. Bingley eventually asks Jane to marry him. Everyone is pleased with the news, most especially Mrs Bennet.

Chapter 56: Lady Catherine visits Longbourn and is very rude to Mrs Bennet. Lady Catherine and Elizabeth take a walk in the garden, where Lady Catherine takes the opportunity to warn Elizabeth off marrying Mr Darcy.

Chapter 57: The following day Mr Bennet receives a letter from Mr Collins telling him of a rumour that Elizabeth is engaged to Mr Darcy and tells him of Lady Catherine's great displeasure at the news. The idea of the marriage amuses Mr Bennet and expects that Elizabeth would feel the same way.

Chapter 58: Darcy returns to Longbourn and while on a walk around the grounds with Elizabeth she thanks him for the kindness he has shown to her family when arranging Lydia's marriage to Wickham. Darcy asks Elizabeth if her feelings are the same as when they last spoke, the previous April. Elizabeth assures him that her feelings are now very different and after a long conversation, the two of them are happy to have many issues cleared up between them and Elizabeth accepts Darcy's offer of marriage.

Chapter 59: Elizabeth tells her family the news of her impending marriage but is hesitant to find out their reaction. Darcy asks Mr Bennet for Elizabeth's hand in marriage and Jane and her father initially find it difficult to believe that Elizabeth is marrying for love. Initially Mrs Bennet is unpleasantly surprised at Elizabeth's news, however once she works out how financially better off her daughter will be, her opinion changes very quickly.

Chapter 60: Elizabeth and Darcy discuss their initial dislike of one another and the reasons their feelings changed. Elizabeth writes to Mrs Gardiner, Mr Darcy to Lady Catherine and Mr Bennet to Mr Collins, each advising of the engagement. Lady Catherine is so upset at the news that life at Hunsford becomes unbearable and the Collinses go to stay at Lucas Lodge. Mrs Phillips and Mr Collins behave so appallingly that Elizabeth looks forward to leaving for Pemberley.

Chapter 61: The final chapter is consumed with the two weddings. Mr Bennet misses Elizabeth greatly and visits her frequently. The Bingleys find that living so close to Longbourn is more than the can bear and move closer to Darcy and Elizabeth. Kitty spends more time with Jane and Elizabeth and her character is better for it. Lydia asks Elizabeth to have Darcy help Wickham acquire a place at court, but Elizabeth refuses to help, though she provides some financial assistance. Georgina Darcy and Elizabeth become close and Georgina makes her home at Pemberley.

CHARACTERS

Elizabeth Bennet: Elizabeth is the protagonist of the novel and second daughter of Mr and Mrs Bennet. Elizabeth is the most intelligent and sensible of their daughters; she is well read and quick witted, and at times more honest than she should be. Elizabeth has many admirable qualities – most particularly, she is intelligent, honest, virtuous and has a lively wit. However, her short temper means that she makes hasty judgements though her ability to admit her errors does allow her to admit her true feelings for Mr Darcy.

Fitzwilliam Darcy: As the son of a wealthy family and best friend to Charles Bingley, Darcy's finest quality is his generosity, despite this not being immediately obvious to the reader. Wickham describes Darcy's generosity when he says that family pride *"has often led him to be liberal, generous – to give away his money freely, to display hospitality, to assist his tenants and relieve the poor."* Wickham was certainly a beneficiary of this generosity when he married Lydia. Another important aspect of Darcy's character is his ability to act promptly, while others are still discussing a course of action. This is, again, evident in the quick response he shows in dealing with Wickham and Lydia's marriage. While initial reactions to Darcy's manners were disagreeable, as the novel moves one, the reader finds he is the epitome of the courteous gentleman.

Jane Bennet: Jane Bennet is often said to be the closest fictional character to Jane Austen's sister Cassandra. While not as forthright as Elizabeth, Jane is nevertheless a charming person who is hesitant to think ill of anyone. Jane is thought to be the prettiest of the Bennet daughters and there is no one in the novel surprised to find Bingley attracted to her. Her kind nature is evidenced regularly in the book, in particularly in her opinion of Charlotte Lucas choosing to marry Mr Collins – *"Jane confessed herself a* *little surprised at the match; but she said less of her astonishment than of her earnest desire for the happiness."* Lydia's marriage to Wickham also brings to light Jane's sympathetic nature, as she finds redeeming features in the unfortunate situation. Jane's humility is rewarded at the end of the book in her finding happiness in being reunited with Bingley and marrying him.

Charles Bingley: Mr Bingley is one of the most affable and likeable people in *Pride and Prejudice*. He is kind and courteous to everyone and seems one of the only people to tolerate Mrs Bennet without showing signs of boredom. Despite his positive features, he is a rather bland character to whom the reader never gets to know very well beyond his relationship ups and downs with Jane.

Mr Bennet: Mr Bennet is largely drawn in relation to how he deals with everyone else in the novel. He obviously finds his wife exasperating, but nevertheless he deals with her with a unique blend of patience and sarcasm. Mr Bennet does have a good appreciation of character and holds his two older daughters – Elizabeth in particular – in high esteem. Having said that, he recognizes that his two younger daughters are possibly *"two of the silliest girls in the country."* It takes Lydia's elopement for him to realize he should have played a more active role in the development of their character.

Mrs Bennet: Mrs Bennet lives to have her daughters married well and her favourite pastime is visiting her neighbours and getting the latest news. Her greatest joy – and achievement – is Jane and Elizabeth's engagement to Bingley and Darcy respectively. Despite the disgraceful way in which Lydia found herself married, she is also very pleased to have a daughter married at the age of sixteen. Mrs Bennet is so obsessed with her daughters' future marriages that even the dull Mr Collins seems a reasonable option and is angry when Elizabeth refuses his offer. Mrs Bennet conversational abilities often embarrass her daughters and are the result of her husband's cynical approach to her and their marriage. Regardless of her bad manners and inappropriate conversation, the reader tends to laugh have a laugh at her expense rather than dislike her.

Lydia Bennet: As the youngest of the Bennet daughters, Lydia is a silly unprincipled teenager, who's life is looking to resemble her mother's. Lydia is the instigator of misbehaving and misdeeds undertaken by herself and her sister Kitty.

Mary Bennet: The reader sees little of Mary throughout the novel, but we are nevertheless aware of her presence. Mary is the middle daughter and is bookish and pedantic. It is Mary that provides moralistic view of the other Bennet girls' activities throughout the novel.

Kitty Bennet: Kitty is very like her sister Lydia, though not as boisterous. Kitty is described in the novel as "delicate" but by the end of the novel, having spent less time in the company of Lydia, her other sisters describer has as "less irritable, less ignorant and less insipid."

Mr Collins: is heir to the Longbourn Estate. Within the novel Mr Collins is described as "a mixture of pride and obsequiousness, self-importance and humility." This is evidenced in his proposal of marriage to Elizabeth and in explaining his reasons for choosing to marry and his inability to comprehend that Elizabeth is sincere in her refusal. He evidently gets over her refusal quickly, though, as Mr Collins quickly becomes engaged to Elizabeth's close friend, Charlotte Lucas. Mr Collins has a parasitic relationship with Lady Catherine de Bough and the way in which he interacts with her only highlights his obnoxious character.

Wickham: is a sociable, charming and fashionable officer who is completely without morals. He moves easily among society and attracts the hearts of many young ladies. Wickham uses his powers of persuasion to convince Elizabeth that he has suffered at the hands of Darcy in order to gain her affections.

Charlotte Collins: is a lovely girl who shocks the reader by agreeing to marry Mr Collins. She deals well with her husband, and while remaining polite, does not cowtail to him. Charlotte explains her reasoning for marrying Mr Collins to her friend Elizabeth by saying *"I am not romantic, I never was. I ask only a comfortable home; and considering Mr Collins' character, connections and situation in life, I am convinced that my chance of happiness with him is as fair as most people can boast on entering the marriage state."* Charlotte recognizes the likeable aspects of her husband's character and deals with it by ignoring his many *faux pas* and encourages him to cultivate his garden in order to obtain relief from his company.

Miss Bingley: has the strong desire to marry Mr Darcy and takes every opportunity to attack Elizabeth's character while at Mr Darcy's presence. She is an ill-natured and spiteful woman, which is evidenced time and again in her treatment of Elizabeth and Jane.

Lade Catherine de Bourgh: thinks of only her own position within society. She regularly provides advice when she is not asked for it and is envious of any accomplishments of ladies younger than herself.

THEMES

Marriage: is largely the principal theme of the novel. In the era in which the novel was written, marriage provided respectability and security. Mrs Bennet's desire to see her daughters marry well conflicts with Charlotte Lucas' practical approach to the institution.

Jane Austen deals with a variety of different aspects of marriage within *Pride and Prejudice*. Austen finds romantic endings for Jane and Elizabeth; marriages of convenience as seen with that of Mr Collins and Charlotte; marriages of indifference witnessed in the marriage of Mr and Mrs Bennet and the disastrous marriage – that of Wickham and Lydia,

Wickham is a prime example of a man that should not marry. He is manipulative and exploits those ladies that develop feelings for him. By marrying Wickham, Lydia has condemned herself to a life of misery as there will never be enough money to cover the cost of the lifestyle they both desire.

Mr Bingley and Mr Darcy act as a stark contrast to Wickham's attitude towards women. Both men are ideal gentlemen with gracious manner and actions that are motivated by love. Austen was quite forward thinking in her modern interpretation of marriage and providing examples of successful and happy marriages based on love in the example of Darcy and Elizabeth and Bingley and Jane.

First Impressions: the original title of the novel indicates one of the main themes and shows how first impressions can be mistaken and should not be long-lasting.

Darcy is a prime example of how deceptive first impressions can be within the initial period of acquaintance. When he is introduced to the readers and the local society at Meryton where his arrogance is evident and he pales in comparison to the charming Mr Bingley. Darcy is rude, refused to mingle and dance and manages to insult Elizabeth while at the dance. However, throughout the novel, it becomes evident that Darcy is nothing but goodness personified towards those he knows and loves.

Wickham is another perfect example of misconstrued first impressions. Initially Elizabeth is quite taken with Wickham, but it is only after her visit to Pemberley, that Elizabeth is made aware of Wickham's true nature.

Love: *Pride and Prejudice* is ultimately a great love story, and the reader is invited to experience the emotion through the two central couples. Despite the obvious romantic love within the novel, there is an apparent lack of passion. Love is in the form of desire is evident in the relationship between Lydia and Wickham. However, the relationship between Elizabeth and Darcy is a love based on intelligence and a spirited nature. The marriage of Jane and Bingley is probably the only one in the novel that is based on a more simplistic idea of love.

www.ingramcontent.com/pod-product-compliance
Ingram Content Group UK Ltd.
Pitfield, Milton Keynes, MK11 3LW, UK
UKHW020228250726
13967UKWH00001B/254